OPEN DOORS

Poems and Stories

That Help You Overcome the Challenges of Life

By Sonya Daniels-Hines

OPEN DOORS: Poems and Stories That Help You Overcome the Challenges of Life.

Copyright ©2023 Sonya Daniels-Hines. All rights reserved.

No part of this publication may be reproduced, distributed, or transmitted in any form or by any means, including photocopying, recording, or other electronic or mechanical methods, or any information storage and retrieval system, without the prior written permission of the author or publisher, except in the case of brief quotations embodied in critical reviews and certain other commercial uses permitted by copyright law. For permission requests, write to the publisher at sony2b@girwomenpower.com.

Library of Congress Control Number: 2023920424

ISBN: 979-8-9872455-0-7 (softcover)
ISBN: 979-8-9872455-1-14 (eBook)

Published by Sonya Daniels-Hines
Edited by Naomi Books, LLC
Printed in the United States of America

DEDICATION

To My Beloved Parents:

Your unwavering support, encouragement, and love have been the foundation upon which I built this book. Thank you for always believing in me, even when I doubted myself. This work is dedicated to you with boundless gratitude.

To My Spouse, My Anchor, and My Muse:
You have been my compass, guiding me through life's storms. Your unwritten words echo in every chapter, and your love fills every page. This book is as much yours as it is mine.

To My Children:
May you always find courage in the face of closed doors. May this book inspire you to seek out new paths, embrace challenges, and discover the magic that lies beyond. You are my greatest adventure.

To the Readers:
Thank you for opening these pages. May they lead you to unexpected places, spark curiosity, and remind you that every door holds a story waiting to be explored.

CONTENTS

Dedication iii

Preface ix

Acknowledgments x

Introduction xii

The Curiosity Of Life 14

Psalm 46:10 16

Faces 17

The Tears Of Sorrow 18

A Young Girl's Cry 20

Walking In My Shoes 22

A Pot Of Good Stuff 23

Congratulations, Friend 24

Chuck-A-Chuck Boom 26

What Goes Around Comes Around 28

Check To Check 30

Dd 911 Equals Death And Destruction 32

Dd 911 33

Time 35

A No-Name Poem 37

A Letter 38

The Fatherless Child	39
Purple Evelina Fields	41
Mother	42
Crack, Baby, Crack	43
Wake Up	45
Son Of Disguise	47
Love Thyself	49
Keeping It Real	50
Greedy	51
Spirit Of Colors And Fruit	53
Soft Whispers	54
Tricky Little Games	55
In Between Races	57
I Love To Eat	59
My Piano	61
Listen	63
The Fight	64
Still	65
Needless To Say	66
Golden Years	67
Mismatched Socks	68
Mr. Bojangles	69
Grudges	71

My Prayer To God 72
The Five Stages Of Death 73
Wounds Healed 75
Life Of A Chair 76
Until Hell Freezes Over 77
I've Never Seen The Righteous Forsaken 78
God's Response 79
Falcons 81
Innocent Eyes 82
Corona 83
The Devil Keeps Watching 85
Old Bones 86
Psalm 91 88
Jeremiah 29:11-14 90
Daughters 91
Wrong Vibes 92
Trippin 93
Jewels & Rags 94
The Shuffled Cards 95
Photos On The Wall 96
Love Warmth Soul 97
Starry Night Over The Rhône 98
Let There Be Light 99

He Rose Again	100
Yesteryears	102
Sonnet: Love B	103
Sonnet: By Mouth	104
Blaze Chaise	105
The Tenant	106
Starstruck	107
Functions	109
God Is Coming Back	111
The Silence Of Time	112
Friends Speak	113
It's Her Right	114
In Death's Doorway	115
Day At The Library	118
The Experiment	124
Burning Secret	126
Burning Secret	128
A Father's Betrayal	129
A Father's Betrayal	131
Restaurant Zero	132
Restaurant Zero	136
Hope	137

PREFACE

In the quiet corners of our lives, there exist portals—thresholds that beckon us toward uncharted territories. These are the *Open Doors*, the gateways to transformation, healing, love, letting go, and self-discovery.

In this captivating book of poetry and short stories, we encounter many stages of life that we must pass through. Our journey unfolds against a backdrop of human experiences and the relentless pursuit of truth and self-discovery. Throughout our journey, we step through each door:

- *The Door of Possibility*: swung open, revealing a path illuminated by hope and endless potential.
- *The Door of Memory*: reflecting on the past... creaking open, spilling forth a whirlwind of forgotten echoes and vivid recollections.
- *The Door of Courage*: sturdy and weathered, it challenges us to face and confront our fears and forge ahead.
- *The Door of Connection*: swinging wide, it introduces kindred souls, unexpected allies, and the fragile threads that bind us all.
- *The Door of Creativity*: beckons with vibrant colors and swirling shapes, promising the realm of boundless imagination and artistic expression.

ACKNOWLEDGMENTS

On the journey of creating *Open Doors*, I've been fortunate to receive support, encouragement, and inspiration from remarkable individuals. Their unwavering belief in this project has been my guiding light.

With heartfelt gratitude, I extend my thanks to:

My Family: To my parents, who instilled in me a love for storytelling, and to my siblings, who cheered me on every step of the way.

My Friends: For their late-night brainstorming sessions, honest feedback, and endless cups of coffee.

My Editor and Collaborators: To the talented souls who shaped this manuscript, your keen eyes and thoughtful suggestions elevated it beyond my imagination.

My Publishers and Production Team: Your dedication to quality and detail transformed words into a tangible reality.

My Mentors and Teachers: You imparted wisdom, challenging my assumptions and nurturing my growth as a writer.

My Inspirations: The women who shattered glass ceilings, defied norms, and paved the way for generations to come.

And also, to every reader who opens these pages, may you find solace, courage, and a sense of belonging. Together, let's keep opening doors, one story at a time.

INTRODUCTION

I am Sonya Hines, the founder of GIRWOMENPOWER.com, the conclusive platform for girls and women who want to reach higher, make a difference, and shine.

I strive to help girls and women reach their full potential through education, self-awareness, and entrepreneurship.

This is a book of poetry and fiction.

Thank you for joining me on this journey. Together, let us discover how to transform our lives through higher education, empowerment, and the tools to succeed!

For we brought nothing into this
world, and it is certain
we can carry nothing out.

— I Timothy 6:7
King James Version

THE CURIOSITY OF LIFE

Is life real, or is it a game?
Have you thought about that,
or did you leave it the same?
It may be a game that everyone plays,
or it might be a rumor that everyone says.

Will we play this game every day?
Or will we live by this rumor everyone says?
Will this game end in joy and laughter?
Or will it end in pain and disaster?

Will this rumor go on from year to year,
or will it end in sorrow and tears?
If this game ends in joy and laughter,
we need not worry about what happens after.

If this rumor goes on from year to year,
we need not worry.
We need not fear.

Life can be confusing; it could also be bold.
With the happenings in it, there's a story to be told.
I'm concentrating hard on this thing called "Life."
The questions keep appearing.
"Is it wrong? Is it right?"

Life is full of good and bad things.
It's up, then down. Mysterious, it seems.
With all the things we experience and feel,
we must ask the question, *"Is life real?"*

PSALM 46:10
King James Version

Be still, and know that I am God:

I will be exalted among the heathen,

I will be exalted in the earth.

FACES

I'm a man of many faces.
I've been around to plenty of places.
I love and respect all races.
Do you know who I am?

I've been with you since the world was created.
I've held your hand when you felt betrayed.
I eased the pain when you felt frustrated.
Do you know who I am?

I taught you to love and only speak the truth.
I watched you grow from a child to your youth.
In the toughest of times, I brought you through.
Do you know who I am?

I blow through your air each day that you rise.
I show to you triumph so it can make you wise.
I give you my love without any ties.
Do you know who I am?

THE TEARS OF SORROW

These tears I cry are not just for you.
I shed them for the hurt and things *I* go through.
Tears because I miss you; they fall with great pain.
Although life goes on, it will never be the same.

No one could understand the depths of my sorrow,
getting through tonight for a better tomorrow.
I may smile, but behind it lies grief.
Friends come and go; there's just no relief.

These tears that I cry are not just for you.
I shed them for the hurt and things *I* go through.
If I could trade places to be where you are...
I know you're listening, and you're not that far.

The hurt has taken over the walls of my pain.
Although life goes on, it will never be the same.
So many things remind me of you
and the unique little things you sometimes like to do.

I am strong, but my emotions are weak.
These are the times that make me weep.
These tears that I cry are not just for you.
I shed them for the hurt and things I go through.

I can take the pain, but my cup is at the top;
a switch for my emotions; I'll turn it to stop.
My mind is weary; my friends are few.
I don't want them around; they haven't a clue.

I need to be alone to sort through the grief.
I'll smile again; wait and see.

~ ~ ~ ~ ~ ~

A YOUNG GIRL'S CRY

Please close your eyes,
and hold your head up toward the sky.
Feel my words as I walk you through a young girl's cry.
Feel my heart's pain as I journey through this path.

I am young and decided to leave home.
Now that I did, I'm scared and alone.

Did you look into my eyes at that last rest stop?

I am staring in a place no one else can see.
I hope and beg from my heart
that someone will rescue me.

I miss my mother, my brother, and my peeps.
I often wonder if they miss me.
I am growing up fast, taking a gamble with life.
He said he loved me and would make me his wife.

Five years later, I'm still in the game.
My body is ruined and will never be the same.
I can say I'm not in the best health,
unrecognizable to myself.

I wanted to love but instead got trapped.
I'm afraid there's no way for me ever to go back.
I was looking for love but soon got played.
My dreams and hopes just faded away.
I reached out for help and nearly got killed.
To the pimps and sex traffickers, it's a laugh or a thrill.

Please try to find me.

I leave notes all around
to get law enforcement to take their asses down.

Signed by:

Your Niece, Brother, Sister, or Friend.

~ ~ ~ ~ ~ ~

WALKING IN MY SHOES

There's something about walking in my shoes.
To trade with me, you shouldn't choose.
My shoes have been through many miles,
not to mention all the different styles
that have come and gone and come back again.
They've been through sand, rain, and wind.

People laugh, but I keep on walking
as the soles tear more, they start to stalling.
I say, "Come on, shoes, just a few more feet!
You bought me through snow, hail, and sleet.
You traveled many years throughout my life.
You've been good to me, like a blade to a knife.

I'm growing old in age, so are you,
but you took me to places I expected you to.
Of all the things I may have bought or used,
you were the *best* old pair of shoes."

A POT OF GOOD STUFF

I will take some hocks and pinto peas,
dice a little onion and garlic leaves.
Put it on to simmer and cook real slow.
When my man comes home, that good stuff flows.

A pot of love cooked and seasoned to my touch.
A warm tub of water says, "I love you so much."
We listen to slow jams as we prepare to eat.
I get out the foot soaker for his tired, aching feet.

My man said, "Baby, dinner smells great.
The aroma is so strong that I can hardly wait."
He told me the biscuits are golden, like pieces in life.
"I'm a blessed man to have you for a wife."

I'm sitting on high because of my Father up above.
A potluck dinner bought a whole lot of love.
A meal for five dollars—it's extremely rich in taste.
That will keep a smile on my good man's face.

CONGRATULATIONS, FRIEND

Let me tell you about those "so-called friends."
They hang around you again and again.
They zap your energy like a negative transformation.
And if you think about it, they have no conversation.

Friends don't come the same.
They're full of lies and malicious games.
They seem to want everything you've grown
instead of going out to get their own.
They envy your man, your home, your car.
They despise your freedom
because they're trapped in a jar.

They watch you vigorously with that stupid stare,
plotting the next part of your life they can tear.
They can't touch you with a ten-foot pole.
They've lost their touch; they have no control.
You helped them out time and time again;
You say to yourself, *they're not my friend.*

They talk and belittle you when your back is turned.
A little voice asks, "Will you ever learn?"
A smile is a frown turned upside down.
You're better off without them following you around.
You're highly favored, and they are not.
Why do you think they want what you got?

You know in your heart they're not genuine.
Break them off! It's way past time.
Do that thing, and don't look back.
Your *real* true friends will have your back.
Smile with ease with no regrets;
be done with the first and last time you met.

They're like chickenpox, irritating and itchy.
Every time you speak, they're cranky and bitchy!
Promise yourself to throw the friendship away.
Don't wait any longer. Do this today!

Now you've overcome a challenging situation.
From me to you, "Congratulations!"

~ ~ ~ ~ ~ ~

CHUCK-A-CHUCK BOOM

I met a man with a chuck-a-chuck boom.
The car looks like something from a cartoon.
It's classic in its time, with a body of rust.
When you open the door—debris and dust.

The horn is broken, the gas gauge too.
How he started that car, I haven't a clue!
Don't judge a man by his car or his tools.
This is a fact from Chuck-a-Chuck Boom.

He earned his name from years of running.
When he turns the corner, you'd hear him coming.
Chuck-a-chuck boom! Chuck-a-chuck boom!
Then he'd let out this very loud *Vroom!*

A collector's item—he's old and antique.
The utmost respect when he's out on the street.
He may be old, but he's plenty of fun.
Chuck-a-Chuck Boom gets the job done.

Don't judge a man by his car or his tools
This is a fact from Chuck-a-Chuck Boom.
His huge toolbox sits deep in the trunk.
Every bump he hits, they rumble and jump.

Anything that breaks, Chuck is aware.
He never goes anywhere unprepared.
Don't judge a man by his car or his tools.
This is a fact from a Chuck-a-Chuck Boom.

Chuck is tight with every bolt and screw.
New cars can't do the things Chuck can do.
Like a fine wine, he's aged with time.
He'll always remain a friend of mine.

~ ~ ~ ~ ~ ~

WHAT GOES AROUND COMES AROUND

I work a job; it's a messed-up place.
People will discriminate right in your face.
I plead the fifth try not to get involved.
If you have a problem, it won't get solved.

Bosses are liars and try to make rules;
they are a disgrace to society, uncaring fools.
They hide *their* mistakes while
shining the light on others.
What's done in the dark will come
from under the covers.

Revealed the truth from an unspoken shame.
Look in the mirror, and that's who you blame.
Singling me out because your position's higher...
you're nothing but a two-faced, backstabbing liar.

You give me your word, then pretend you forgot;
when you fall on your face, I hope you rot.
I have no respect for what you've done.
I heard you couldn't take it, so you're out on the run.

You shouldn't have to run if you know you're right;
you should stand tall and try to fight.
You fight with the position giving you power;
that's why you're dismissed this very hour.

Funny how life's tables turn.
Out of your chaos, I hope you learned.
You made this bed, so simply lay down.
Remember, what goes around comes back around.

CHECK TO CHECK

I'm so tired of living check to check.
I feel like a rope is around my neck,
and each day that passes, the rope gets tighter.
But I won't give up. I'm a natural-born fighter.
My table is stacked and filled with bills;
to open them up gives me chills.

Gas, lights, cable, and phone;
I wish they all would just leave me alone.
I can pay some now, but not the whole thing;
all day long, my telephone rings.
When, where, what, and why...
I'm so frustrated I want to cry.
Insurance: home, life, and car.
My next payday is not that far.

They're so impatient; they just can't wait.
They call so I can confirm the date.
Now, what gets me is they don't stop there;
the next person calls, saying,
"Your payments are not here!"
Visa, Mastercard, Discover Card, too.
Well, I cut them up because I'm surely through!

Consolidation companies have run my name,
sending all those letters, drives me insane.
I must owe every bank across the west.
I can truly say I have been put through the test.

Those credit cards are not for me.
If I don't have cash, I'll let it be.
I got on my knees and prayed one day
for my Heavenly Father to take them away.
Once He did, it taught me the law.
I never needed those cards at all!

Now, I'm not living check-to-check.
That rope was removed from off my neck.
Now I feel as if I can breathe;
I might not be rich, but I *am* relieved.

~ ~ ~ ~ ~ ~

DD 911 EQUALS DEATH AND DESTRUCTION

Attack on our Country

Total death and deceit.
Suppose you were to leave a letter explaining this day.

Death came to visit many citizens, workers,
and children—all unexpected.

A private war set up by terrorism to destroy
the souls of thousands of people.
Innocent people had gone to work and daycare
with the expectancy of returning home.

Buildings collapsed as the pain of hollering dust
was so thick, you could not escape it.
People on the outside watched and yearned
to help those inside, trapped.

DD 911

My heart aches and breaks as I play back the tape
repeatedly in my mind.
A country so powerful had very little time.

The invaders had come like thieves in the night.
The impact of their destruction was not a good sight.
Tourism took lives without signs;
we all mourned during this terrible time.

Mothers lost daughters and, likewise, the same.
People held pictures as they yelled out in pain.
Children lost their parents with no understanding.
How could this enemy be so demanding?

They didn't give a damn about the lives they took!
As the planes hit the building, the entire ground shook.

The blood of our ancestors was buried in dust,
but we, as Americans, *Dear God we trust.*
The smell of flesh burning, the winds of sorrow;
Limited! Thoughts of getting to tomorrow?
Our hearts are crushed!
A foolish sneak attack.
Issues should have been discussed.
No! You went behind our backs.

DD 911, you made our Book of Shame.
You smirk and grin because your dirty work is done;
there's no one but you to blame.
Now, you run and hide, cowardly among your peers.
All the money you hold and even *you* have fears.
Next time you see our flag,
the stripes and stars that wave.
Remember, we are America, the Home of the Brave!

To all our fallen soldiers,
you've made our Book of Fame.
When the wind blows,
it will whistle out your names.
We'll set a day aside for prayers
and remembrance of you.
We'll scream out to the world
that you were Americans, too.

We will love you always!
From your fellow Americans.

~ ~ ~ ~ ~ ~

TIME

I am time. I wait on no one, it's true.
You don't scare me; I scare you.
I make you rush, worry, and cry.
I don't have time to explain why.

Time: It's time to stop comparing me with the devil;
I'm too fast for him and won't stoop to his level.
You will never see me, but pay attention to my tracks.
You'll wonder where the time went,
and you'll want it back.

I don't give in to those puppy-dog, sad eyes.
I can't hear you... only your cries.
I am anti-emotional and can feel nothing.
Come on, people, bet your money on something.

I make you stay when you know you should have left.
I am time; there *is* nothing else.
I caught up with you when you tried to get away.
You wondered to yourself where the time went today.

I am time, in and out, without a trace.
You will meet me sometime, someplace.
I am time, and my tracks don't stop.
You can turn me off, but I'll remain at the top.

It's time for you to accept who and what I am.
My possibilities are endless; some call me their friend.
I don't have friends because no bargains do I give.
I will keep you wondering—with no alternatives.

I control your life whether you like it or not.
You go by *my* time, and that's all you've got.
Spend your time wisely because
there won't be much to spare.
When I strike, you'll know... I've been there.

~ ~ ~ ~ ~ ~

A NO-NAME POEM

This will be a not-so-sad poem—a not-even-mad poem.
An I-don't-care-if-you-like-it-or-not poem.
This is *my* poem.
Whatever you want, make it *your* poem!

I write what I feel, and I think what I write.
I don't care about the media and its critical hype.
It's all the same, and they judge *me*.
The Fifth Amendment gave me the freedom to speak.
I'm writing it down, but I can see it's so clear.
Destruction, government, and homeless people appear.

Now, this pulls back from being a sad poem
and most definitely told not to be a mad poem.
There is bias, money, schemes and theft,
the deficit, welfare prisons, and poor health.
All different issues, yet the problems are the same.
Lies, truth, a gold digger's game.

The things we can't see when the blinds are down.
The noise is loud, yet you can't hear the sound.
Some of the biggest thieves wear ties and suits.
Some pretend to be poor yet have crazy loot.

A LETTER

Why have they taken the Almighty out of the schools?
Now, teenagers are disrespectful and somewhat rude.
They do what they want, leaving room to slack.
Well, I say it's time to bring prayer back.
Say a two-minute prayer with the Pledge of Allegiance.
This can be done throughout all the regions.

Prayer worked years ago. I read it in a letter,
and back in those days, things were better.
We didn't hit teachers or blow up the schools.
We did what we were told; we followed the rules.
We had a prayer to start our day.
We didn't lash out when we couldn't get our way.

Praying to our Almighty could make our children better.
I know it for myself because I read it in a letter.
Our children are lost, so they turn to destruction.
Who has failed them, causing hate and corruption?
Prayer should be allowed with no questions asked.
They take it away, and kids get too relaxed.

They're out of control!
Smart-mouthed and bold.
Prayer would be best.
Tension would be less.
Let's bring it back.
It's time to act.

THE FATHERLESS CHILD

The child was fatherless because he chose to be.
A whole lot of love is what he missed from me.
I tried to reach out to be on his side.
He wouldn't accept. At least I tried.
I have my own money, so I don't need his.
Throughout his life, he's been misled.
He is told that cash is what I am after.
Was it worth spending life as a fatherless bastard?

The divorce was fatal, affecting my child.
Many court battles and numerous papers filed.
I took a divorce from my wife, not my son.
But in *her* mind, she thinks she's won.
She taught him to hate and look the other way.
I will come out with my son one day.

(Now he's grown.)
A fatherless son is what he's become.
It's not my fault; he rejects his name.
For many years, I took the blame,
and when he hurt, I felt his pain.

All I ever wanted was him in my life.
All I ever received was broken strife.
His mother was determined to keep him to herself,
drilling in his head—money and wealth.

He has siblings he has never seen,
holding grudges in his heart
when they're from the same team.
He was taught hate, and that's not from God.
His mother spoiled the child and spared the rod.

Now he's grown and believes I didn't care.
I made numerous attempts to try to be there.
The door has been slammed right in my face.
A father-son relationship becomes a terrible waste.

A piece of my spirit will remain in his soul.
There are two sides to a story that will one day be told.
I am so glad that God is my judge.
He taught me to love and let go of the grudge.

~ ~ ~ ~ ~ ~

PURPLE EVELINA FIELDS

I am passing through the most critical period of my life.
Again and again, I have asked myself these questions:

Why have I failed at so many things?
Is it based on selfishness? Love? Am I a fool?
Do I not give enough of myself?
What is it to love someone and know I have loved them?

For the second time in my life, I became jealous—jealous of
someone else, and the sad thing about it
was that the person didn't even know me.

Do I not have compassion? Have I betrayed anyone?
Have I no regrets?

I feel so alone.

Is there no one in this world for me?
Will I ever find love?

I went to the hospital today.
I visited a friend who is dying.

What do you say to someone who knows they are dying?

I see life and death every day.
I know so little about one and nothing about the other.

MOTHER

My mother is proud, strong, and loving.
She is caring, giving, and beautiful.
She raised six children to be grown and independent.
My mother taught me about God.
I learned how to go to Him and pray.
I thank Him for life every day.
She gave me all I needed to live.
There is no greater love than my mother's.

CRACK, BABY, CRACK

Another crack baby—just fresh, newly born.
Born in a world that's prejudiced and torn.
Born with a system polluted, not clean.
Born to a mother who treated him mean.
Born with an addiction before taking her first breath.
Hooked up to tools, needles, and machines
without a hope left.

Crack, baby, crack, because you are not to blame.
You scream and holler every half hour;
your throat is sore and inflamed!
The odds are against you
because your mother didn't care.
She ruined *your* life; just like her own.
The outcome isn't fair.

She claimed she was going to stop,
but tomorrow never came.
She smoked, sniffed, took a needle,
and shot it in your veins!
She didn't eat very healthy
to give you the things you need.
As she stands over you crying,
her nose starts to bleed!

Crack, baby, crack, and I'll meet you in heaven.
You weren't the first to die from your mom;
you make crack baby number seven.
Seven little lives so innocent and lost.
With your high-risk habit, your babies paid the cost.
How could you sleep at night?
How could you shut your eyes?
I'd imagine that all you hear are all those little cries!

~ ~ ~ ~ ~ ~

WAKE UP

He comes around to spend some time, just a little while.
You're his only woman
for the short time that you smile.
You don't often smile because soon he has to leave.
He must go home to his wife,
whom he viciously cheats and deceives.
You begin to join the cycle, that this is all cool.
Don't you forget... when it happens to you.

Oh, he says he loves you, and you're his unique jewel.
Think back to the day when *you* broke the golden rule.
You started as friends, then more, I declare.
You both are being selfish, and that just isn't fair...
to the Missus.

He told you he would leave her two times—
then three times—and four.
All you ever see is him walking out the door.
He must return home to the family he once adored.
He tells you he has no time for her
and treats her pretty mean.
You fail to accept the truth that he tells *you*
the same thing.

He tells you that *you're* the best
and no one can take your place.
All your years of nothing were just a total waste.
He tells you that he hates her and doesn't get along.
Why is he still with her then, if nothing is wrong?
You need to stop denying this same old tired track.
Ask God for forgiveness, then claim your life back.

SON OF DISGUISE

I knew it, Son, when I looked in your eyes.
I knew you'd be my son of disguise.
You came with pleasure, heartache, and pain,
and you have the nerve to brag on your name.
I tried so hard to teach you respect, but part of your brain just wouldn't connect.
Barely a man, but *you* know it all.
I stood by your side, fall after fall.

You disrespect me with your nasty, smart mouth.
Everything I taught you, suddenly you doubt.
Your father was absent for more than half your life.
This made me work harder to do things right.
I sacrificed plenty for the things you need.
In return, your words make my heart bleed!

I see my reflection as the water passes by.
I'm giving you to God, and I will not cry.
I was your first teacher, and I taught you well.
Instead, you act like something that burst out of hell.
The devil *is* a liar because I did my best,
working doubles and triples so you wouldn't have less.

You put up a front to make your papa proud,
interrogating my intelligence like I was on trial.
God sits high, and He sees low.
You should act your age; how low can you go?
God has blessed me with all that I have,
and, like anything else, this too shall pass.

You will need Him one day, Son.
You'll see why God keeps on blessing me.
You only pray when you're in need.
But one day, Son, your heart will bleed.
God is near, but you push Him away.
You will scream out His Name someday.
The sun doesn't set and rise on you,
but in your mind, you think that's true.
Your mind has been poisoned and fell into a trap.
I will continue to ask God to bring you back.

~ ~ ~ ~ ~ ~

LOVE THYSELF

You judge me based on credentials,
but you know not who I am.

You look at me and drop your head as if I'm not good enough to be on your roster. I don't appear wealthy or sufficient for you. When you see me, you pretend you don't? You hurt me with your gossip and spread it like a plague. Although you're not cut out to be what you want people to think of you.

You live up to other people's standards. You'll never enjoy life because you don't have one. You are dead to your existence. Everything you do must please other people, yet you look down on me.

Some say you have a beautiful personality, but you are bitter, torn, and confused on the inside. So many people think you're all *that* when in doubt; the scariest thing about it is that many dream of being like you.

Acceptance starts with yourself. Denial is the state that must be admitted. I may not have what you have; however, I'm happy with what I possess.

Blessed is the man who is happy with what he has.

Inner peace is more remarkable than a pot of money.

KEEPING IT REAL

When I think of my existence,
I look up to the sky and thank my Father.

"That's keeping it real."

When life's frustration overwhelms the rinse cycle,
I will come out squeaky clean.

"That's keeping it real."

I will remain firm and unbreakable
when you whisper and pierce my soul.

"That's keeping it real."

When your Sugar Daddy runs out of things to give, mine will remain to stand, teaching me to keep it accurate. When the *jones* that keeps up with the Joneses is trying to figure out my life, I will remain rich in spirit and prosperity. When I'm down to my last piece of meat, I will not tell you so that you can repeat it.

When the voices of friends have come and gone,
I will be here for you.

With my Almighty Father, you're never alone.

"That's keeping it real."

GREEDY

People of power raised our gas prices,
rolling the dice as if we were lifeless.
They live in a place called *The Millionaires Club.*
It's all about them; they don't show us love.
Now, I'm not angry about their money and fame.
It's the average American they continue to drain.

I can only put half a tank in my car.
We all know that won't take you far.
I won't put my furnace above sixty-eight
because when the gas bill comes,
that's more on my plate.
For one single month, the bill's two nighty-nine.
It's drained my pocket to the very last dime.

For dinner last night, I ate peanut butter and jelly.
I didn't have meat, but it filled my belly.
I turned on the news; another person got shot.
I said to myself; this happens a lot.
Another mother cries... a part of her dies.
So much corruption leads to destruction.

"How can I make it?" I asked myself.
I don't have prestige or wealth.
My Father said, "Live one day at a time."
Put Him first, and I should be fine.
I want to live and pay my bills.
There are so many obstacles, so many hills.
A man can't change the world in four years only.
If you think you can, you're misleading and phony.

SPIRIT OF COLORS AND FRUIT

A young boy and his mother discussed how to teach
his more youthful brother his colors.
He would have to know and use them
throughout his life.
The boy's mother always had a unique way
of explaining whatever he asked.
She would teach other things the same way
she first introduced him to his Bible.
If the boy's mother said, "Seek ye first the kingdom
of God..." he would finish the prayer by saying,
"All things will be added to you."

Remember the B's: blue, brown, and black.
Tar on the ground, and it sticks like sap.
Brown sugar is sweet, and you can pack it real tight.
Blueberry pies as they cool through the night.
Green, like money, could be the root of all evil.
Olives and lettuce could taste good on seafood.

Purple petunias, as they grow out of the ground.
Yellow spirits fly without a sound.
Red, you right, and orange, you sweet.
Dandelions brown as they burn from the heat.
White is pure and like cotton to touch.
Don't ever forget that I love you so much.

SOFT WHISPERS

I sit by you as you take the last few breaths.
So many memories are going through my head.
The soft whispers of the last time we talked.
I am racing against an unbeatable time
that keeps going.

I can't imagine life without you.
In just a few breaths, I will have no choice.
I will forever be filled with the time we spent together.
Then, I will grieve the time that is no more.

There's a new life you are about to encounter
with Jesus in the dwelling place.
The angels must be awaiting your arrival.
I hope there are over ten thousand or more.
I know when you get there, the heavy felt burdens
will be gone.

When the raindrops fall, they can blend
with my tears of sorrow.
I will weep for only a short while because
joy comes tomorrow.

TRICKY LITTLE GAMES

Those tricky little games you always seem to play
will one day turn around and hurt you just the same.
I do not wish upon you the bitterness you bought me.
Experience is the best teacher.

Through experience, you will see that love takes time;
it's nothing you can fix overnight.
Sometimes, it could be beautiful or piercing like a knife.
You let me down with your lying tongue
that deceived me.
I put all the trust I had in you,
and just look at how you treated me.

You sit there looking stupid
with a strange look in your eyes.
I think of all the nights I spent
trying hard not to cry.
I toss and turn, get up, lay down.
I don't know what to do.
All my sleepless, restless nights...
just because of you.

Those tricky little games always brought us down.
When I needed you most, you were not around.

I wonder how you'll take it;
when what you threw gets thrown back at you.
Don't think I will take you back.
When I hate, I never knew you.

IN BETWEEN RACES

I went to the mall to look for some clothing.
Three different people asked, "May I help you?"
"No!" After answering them all,
they went in their separate directions.
The mirror glass across their store revealed faces
with frowns, smirks, and grins.
Why must you make me feel this within?
My money is green and spent like yours,
giving me the right to enter this store.
Oh, I see; you can't figure out my race.
You feel I don't belong in this place.

I continued to shop.
Very softly, I could hear the salespeople saying,
"Is she Black, or is she White?"
"Her skin complexion is kind of light."
My blood *did* boil, and now I'm pretty outraged!
I felt like an animal trapped in a cage.
I shouted, "I came to shop, not argue about my race!
What does it matter the color of my face?"

After their insults and racial slurs,
it all fiercely got on my nerves.
We all should love people from every race,
but from every race, some do disgrace us.
My mother is Black; my father is White.
They said, "We don't judge from one's position or sight."

I am the outcome of two great colors,
but on forms and applications, I'm labeled as "other."
My best friend is Chinese, and my man's Hispanic.
Did your mouth drop open? Did you start to panic?
Race never mattered or tore us apart.
We're friends forever in each other's hearts.

I LOVE TO EAT

I love to eat, and that's my one temptation.
Yeah, I diet—on different occasions.
Kale, greens, chicken, and ham.
Help me, Lord, I'm in a jam.
I partake in a desire to eat things,
especially cabbage and garlic wings.
When I go out, a salad may do,
but I can't help but think about some beefy hot stew.

On Thanksgiving Day, I must leave the earth.
All that good food is what it's worth.
The diet drinks are okay, but I can't help but wish
I was sitting at a table eating lobster and fish.
You all may laugh, and it's a little bit funny
how I relate everything to chicken and honey.
Macaroni and cheese with ribs and steak;
a three-layered strawberry cream puff cake.
I'm a little big with the intention to lose weight.
I just don't know what it will take.

Shakes, pills, and hypnotize—
won't keep those inches off my thighs.
I have tried them, but not for long.
My mind starts wondering if I'm not that strong.
Mashed potatoes with gravy on top.
Roast beef on the side with a nice cold pop.
How can I resist such tasteful things?
I go back to thinking about ham and greens.
Potato salad on a hot summer day,
a plate for later to send me on my way.

Maybe in the future, I'll take my mind off eating.
I'll go on a diet without any cheating.
You be sure and pray for me;
that one day, the Lord will set me free.

~ ~ ~ ~ ~ ~

MY PIANO

When I play my piano,
the sound makes love to my soul.
Each note that I strike has a different sound.
It is so pleasurable to the universe.
The sharp and the low keys were perfectly
lined up like soldiers for war.
A sound of delicacy is yet bold and definite
as it is composure.
Each key that I strike reminds me of phases
of my yesteryears.

My piano is the one thing that brings
me back to a lovely place.
When I'm angry, I play my piano.
When I'm lonely, I play my piano.
When I meditate, I play my piano—
the one thing that brings me back to it all—
notes of sadness, chords of good times.
You will take up no space in my mind
when I play my piano.

As I strike the bars from the base keys,
it sounds like thunder.
My fingers swell as I play a little bit longer.
You may love a man or a woman.
I love my piano.
I once heard there's no greater love than
the instruments of the mind—soothing therapy
and relaxation for the soul.

LISTEN

If you only listen, you will see just what you're missing.
But unfortunately, your mouth is always flapping,
so now your hearing seems to be lacking.

Listen with your ears as you watch with your eyes.
It will make you a better person.
It's sure to make you wise.

You will be surprised by what you learn to keep quiet.
Knowledge would come to you, so why don't you try it?
Be open to listening; it's not that hard to do.
You would be happy if you did
because this would benefit you.

THE FIGHT

I remember my friend and the memories we have.
He had war dispersed in his heart.
His love was gone, and he was my sweetheart.

His heart was departing from his other members.
His eyes were glaring at a place only he could see.
His outlook on life was no longer carefree.

His only delight was ejecting his gun;
the sound of the speed made him run.
Often, I didn't know where he was going.
These changes in him are all mind-blowing.

He stares in deep thought with his gun;
I know he wouldn't hurt anyone.
The system wants to put him in an institution or cage.
They said he is dangerous with hell and rage.

He's been gone fighting a senseless war
and then left all alone like a nasty bed sore.
I remember my friend very differently in his life;
when he got back, I was to become his wife.

He is a man meant to be loving and gentle.
But just like that, he's somewhat mental.
We both suffered a loss as painful as it gets.
In both our hearts beat a tragic regret.

STILL

I'm still, but it feels like I'm moving very fast!
I want it to be silent, but the quietness is too loud.
At delightful times, the sadness is overwhelming.

I'm trying to open my mouth,
but no words will come out.
After that, things will never be the same.
I want to be enraged but can't.
I want to jump up and shout.
Unfortunately, my feet won't let me move.

I want to relax; my mind keeps drifting.
I want to accept help, but I'm too proud to ask.
I want to sob, but my pride won't let me.
I want revenge, but vengeance is not mine.
I want to have energy.

Moreover, I'm restless and edgy.
I want to make motions.
Yet, I'm still like a tree.

NEEDLESS TO SAY

She could be whoever she wants in her mind; it's unfortunate to say she wouldn't mind being anyone but herself.

It's clear to see that she's not excited about some events. The first, her persuasion to walk paths that don't compliment her purpose for being here. Next, her eyes witnessed chaotic wars that would tear your thoughts apart. Finally, a human being or animal should never feel these feelings.

Some of her thoughts are brutal but destined for the life that leads her body. *Is she a superhero?* Maybe. She's less than two worlds apart. In one, she is the mat that keeps it together; in the other world, she has passed all of us on some occasion, helping someone
through difficulties.

Why can't she reveal who she is? To display it can make her weak and useless; her strength comes from not telling anyone who she is. *Can you imagine having a top secret you can't share with anyone?*

Her power is in secrecy.

GOLDEN YEARS

He's reached his golden years by far.
No more walks or trips to the bar.
His teeth are too big, so they slip out of his mouth.
He doesn't like anyone in his house.
His knees hurt as they buckle together.
He told me it's because of the wet, damp weather.
His hair is short with stubby gray whiskers.
He can't sit long because his butt will blister.

Golden years.

They have come at age ninety-nine.
His mind is as good as yours and mine.
So don't ever boss him or take his choice.
You'll never hear the end of his deep, raspy voice.

Golden years.

His back is bent slightly, but he still gets around—
He and his dog, or, as he says, "hound."
He has a girl whom he calls his friend.
He treats her nicely, which is better than most men.

MISMATCHED SOCKS

Where is the other sock?
I washed them together.
Now, my basket is light as a feather.
A few are missing—just disappeared.
I can't find them anywhere.

Now you understand why I wear two different socks.
As long as they're clean, I'm leaving this house.
I can't take time trying to match them the same.
The socks are playing me like a silly board game.

When I come back in, they suddenly appear.
I think I'm going to go have a beer.

MR. BOJANGLES

Mr. Bojangles, what can I say?
You will make somebody's day.
A man of such charisma;
a suit and tie that fit you.

Your shoes are shining so very slick;
Mr. Bojangles, you're a man for the chicks.
When Mr. Bojangles enters a room,
women admire his upkeep and groom.

He makes the most influential women in the room stare.
Come to think about it,
he looks good in anything he wears.
Or should I say whatever wears him?

I will be his biggest fan.
Mr. Bojangles, just let me stare.
Oooh! How you wear your hair!
There isn't much that Bojangles can't do.

He spreads much love to me and you.
Mr. Bojangles won't settle for less;
he looks good with his big, broad chest.
A man who makes you inhale and hold.
He's not shy; he's flashy and bold.

When he passes, I can't help but see
some possibilities between him and me.
Hmmm, Mr. Bojangles, every woman's wish.
He's better than your best-tasting dish.

When God made man, He made him well.
Mr. Bojangles, you kiss and tell.
If *you* don't tell, then *I* won't tell.
Mr. Bojangles, well, well, well!

~ ~ ~ ~ ~ ~

GRUDGES

How long are you going to hold that grudge?

Sooner or later, it will begin to deteriorate
your heart and mind.

Holding grudges keeps you from reaching your true
inspirations in life.

Holding grudges keeps your mind on things
that are not important.

Holding grudges blocks the genuine faith
you have in yourself.

It freezes up your confidence in God.

Holding grudges will keep you in a state
of unsureness and confusion.

Resentment hinders you and blocks your mind from receiving
proper understanding.

MY PRAYER TO GOD

God, I pray for you to break every chain
and link of fear, low finances, family curses,
poor health, and habits.

Please break backbiting, confusion, jealousy, envy,
bondage, uncertainties, unsureness, thieves, and liars.

Please, God, give us peace from You.
May we lift You and glorify You to the fullest.

Thank you for Your Son Jesus,
who died on the cross for our sins.

We ask that You cure this mean virus, COVID.
Please keep us protected from any new virus.
Please protect us from any hurt or danger.

Thank You.

THE FIVE STAGES OF DEATH

Don't get caught up in the Five Stages of Death.
You better do it right now while there's still time left.
Tomorrow is not promised, so you better change fast, because
none of us knows how long our lives will last. Imagine lying on
your deathbed bargaining for time.
Is it the last thing you may have on your mind?

Yes, I've watched it happen time and time again;
people deny death right to the end.
They know they must accept it and take what's coming.
As they review their lives, they know
they are running...
out of time... as it draws the family nearer.
Death is something coming,
although it makes us *all* inferior.

Death means the end; no more, all gone.
You may have been a person who didn't
do much wrong.
You may be a person who's stuck on your wealth;
the Five Stages of Death will take your health.
You may show anger, and that will pass soon.
You may buy an expensive doctor
who can't mend the wound
of the Five Stages you know are coming.
You refuse to believe, and your mind

keeps you running.

You'll slow down to bargain for time;
this can't be bought, so it burdens your mind.
You think of other answers, but time is running out.
You think of all the damage you have done
and try to sort it out.

When you get down to it, there's not enough time.
You never thought it could happen to you;
you think you've lost your mind.
Of course, it's not your mind you're losing;
it's your life, and you're afraid.
Finally, however, you must lie down
in this bed you made.
The Five Stages of Death are no joke.
It's for real.

~ ~ ~ ~ ~ ~

WOUNDS HEALED

Moving on with you is all that is important.
I have waited; it seems an eternity for this day to come.
Moving on with you, my beginning, and my purpose.
My love, we will become one in love
in my heart and soul.

I never thought that happiness would revisit my heart.
You, and only you, are the essential element
of my living.
You are the part that makes me complete.

The ghosts and the demons made me believe love
was a good thing for a short while; then came you.
Right then and there, destinies meet.
You have healed the wounds of my heart:
no more ghosts or uncertainties.

Because of you, we can look forward
to our future of greatness.
We will jump hurdles; we will jump and climb together.
It will be you and me forever.
I love you, crave you, and accept you.

My heart and soul say, "I love you."

LIFE OF A CHAIR

Have you ever thought about the life of a chair?
All the butts we hold; it's not fair.
Big butts, little butts, and huge butts too.
No one would believe what a chair goes through.
Sitting in your den. By you, we are not fazed.
We are sick and tired, and we all want a raise.
And not the raise of a rag dusting us down.

If it weren't for us, you'd be sitting on the ground,
the floor, or the rug, whichever you please.
We are something crucial that everyone needs.
People sit on us and blow hot air.
Kids have accidents; now, is that fair?
If we go on strike, to keep your butts off us,
we'll call the couches and loveseats to come join us.

Now, you'd look mighty strange typing standing up;
standing at the breakfast table drinking from your cup;
standing at the movies, trying to watch the show.
So, we thought we'd speak our minds
and let the world know.

UNTIL HELL FREEZES OVER

You thought this would be a nicey-nice song—
until hell freezes over. Again, you're wrong.
You've been headstrong your entire life long
Just let me sing my country song.
You worked my nerves until they were gone.
I want to sing a lovely swan song.

You and I don't belong.
Until hell freezes over, leave me alone.
All you do is fuss and groan.
You're on your own; you're a woman scorned.
Until hell freezes over, shut your blabbermouth.
Pack your bags and perhaps head south.
I'm fed up and ready to bounce;
you drained me down to my last ounce.

Sometimes I ask if hell *will* freeze over.
You remind me of a broken recorder.
Repeat line one in that exact order,
then pack your things and head to the border.

I'VE NEVER SEEN THE RIGHTEOUS FORSAKEN

Lord, here I call again, another trying day at work. Everything that went wrong, of course, had something to do with me. *My nerves are jumping with fear because someone almost ran me off the road!* This raggedy old car is on its last ride and desperately needs work.

Kids are acting up in school; Mark cut his classmate's ponytails off. The gas bill is four hundred ninety-nine dollars. *Where will I get the money to pay it?*

My best friend is on the phone complaining about her man. My brother stopped by and asked to borrow twenty dollars. *I need that for tomorrow's dinner.*

Lord, I know you don't like complainers, but I need some help! Sometimes I feel like giving up.

I can't help but wonder if I will ever see the light at the end of the tunnel.

GOD'S RESPONSE

My dear child, I'm pleased you call on me;
be humble so you can call on me.
Remember, everything that seems wrong is not wrong.
If you start to have fear,
immediately replace it with faith.

I will clothe you in my entire armor.
Your car may be raggedy and old, but ask yourself, "Didn't it start up and take you to your job, doctor's appointment, or destination?" Remember three years ago, when you did not have a license to drive and bring more understanding to this situation? Wasn't it you who
called yourself the "bus," "train," or "Uber queen?"

I know sometimes children act up in school.
At least they're in school.
When you stated that the gas bill is high, be grateful that you have a home that has gas.
You said you didn't know where you
would get the money.

Did you forget I'm your Almighty Father?
I own everything on this earth.
Did you get so caught up in the daily activities
that you forgot how to come to me and pray?

Your best friend is on the phone complaining
about her man; unless she wants to change things,
you certainly can't.
Sometimes, my dear, you forget to concentrate on
your life, making other people's problems yours.

When it seems like you have very little money,
I know how you feel, especially when someone
important in your life needs it for their emergency.
I taught you not to worry about what you will
eat, drink, or wear.

When you put me first,
I have already taken care of all your needs.

Do you have any questions?

No, I don't, but I want to thank You.
I love You.
Please come and talk to me again.
Have Your way, Lord.

~ ~ ~ ~ ~ ~

FALCONS

I remember the days I tried to do well with you.
You shattered my hopes and desires.
You, the one person I thought understood
my thoughts and visions.
You blind me like a chemical.

I made you feel that life without you was impossible; you made
me believe in nonexistence.
I tried to overlook the remorseful times.
You, the constant reminder.
I stood up for you when so many others
ridiculed your name.
You put me down so low; the dirt from the earth
thought I was its grandmother.

When I ponder you, I think of vultures, birds of prey.
Most birds have free spirits with a song to sing.
I will pray for you because you are a falcon.

INNOCENT EYES

Innocent eyes have seen too much in a lifetime;
their backs have deteriorated with broken blood vessels.
Each blink reveals an unwanted memory.

The small wrinkles reveal age and secrets.
The inside of the eye reveals the pulps that lost their way. The iris flashes short scenes of an unknown path.
The sclera is no longer white;
it's faded, dull, and yellowish.

Innocent eyes seem jumpy and nervous.
Anyone will admit that they've been through wars
and tragedy; then they blink
another memory of some sad scene.

Unfortunately, this is not a fix for an eye doctor.

CORONA

You are small but grew large.
You came to our world to show you are in charge.
You wreck lives, took a thousand souls;
continuous tests going up our nose.
You shut us down, our schools and stores.
We couldn't keep up; we soon grew poor.
We had to close with no money to pay;
worldwide in one sad day!

Symptoms spread from place to place;
record high numbers case by case.
Stimulus went out to boost our economy.
Who do we blame—the real democracy?
Believe it or not, things started to improve.

Corona Virus, you're hateful and cruel.
Killing people while taking their strength,
charging them guilty as if they're on the bench.
You have killed adults, babies, and kids,
breaking our spirits like branches and twigs.

Leave our existence to leave us alone.
We want to go back to a place called home.
Hospitals are full, so the family can't stay.
I don't know if our families will see another day!

Vaccines and boosters may slow you down,
but we'll fight like hell when you come back around. Body
aches, sneezes—we can hardly breathe.
Fever, headache... I pray that they leave.

There are not enough ventilators to get us all through. You
attacked us by surprise; we didn't know what to do.

So, we'll part here; please let yourself out.
You're never welcome to any of our houses!

~ ~ ~ ~ ~ ~

THE DEVIL KEEPS WATCHING

The devil keeps watching; he wants you to slip.
He waits for you anxiously to lose your grip.
He visits your dreams like a thug in the night.
You see through his eyes; it's a pitiful sight.
He gives you some pills; you soon feel strange.
You smell flesh burning, people hollering in pain.
You pinch yourself as hard as you can;
you can't feel anything. You're still human.

You've entered a tunnel full of smoke and skulls;
you see half-visible people talking mess, doing drugs.
"Am I in hell?" I asked in my mind.
I'm only twenty-four. I thought I had more time.
My mother goes to church; she doesn't miss a beat.
I thought that this would somehow also save me.

A loud voice yelled, "No!"
I want to go back. I wouldn't say I like it here.
Next, I trembled with cries and tears.
Everything was dead; it had no life.
Soon, pieces of my body started to die.
Finally, I asked God for one more chance.
I woke up in my bed in a new circumstance.

OLD BONES

These old bones still cry out.
I heard the ground say, "Shut your mouth."
They are tired but still can't rest;
they've expressed how they're oppressed.

Knees on necks taking his wind.
Now he's not with us. What a sin!

Skittles and iced tea were going to see his pops;
he got ambushed by a wanna-be cop.
That man was told, "Please stand down!
You're not the law; stop following him around."
Just because his skin was brown.
So, he took out his weapon and took him down.

Taking a nice jog, as he did in spare time,
Being murdered by three men
had never crossed his mind!

Lying in her bed, they picked the wrong house.
Did they investigate correctly? I seriously doubt.

These old bones lay deep beneath the ground;
they still can't rest due to the chaos of the sound.

A senseless traffic stop mistakes her taser for her gun;
Now, this beautiful mother has to live without her son.

Hands were up high, and he still got shot.
He was only a teen; the bones still cry out.

Playing in the park, the toy wasn't real.
It seems as if you are anxious to draw your steel.

Taking a fun walk with his friend by his side.
There is no way this young man had to die.

Well, the list goes on about these senseless deaths.
These are just a few, so the bones can't rest!

~ ~ ~ ~ ~ ~

PSALM 91
King James Version

He that dwelleth in the secret place of the most High shall abide under the shadow of the Almighty.

I will say of the Lord, He is my refuge and my fortress: my God; in him will I trust.

Surely he shall deliver thee from the snare of the fowler, and from the noisome pestilence.

He shall cover thee with his feathers, and under his wings shalt thou trust: his truth shall be thy shield and buckler.

Thou shalt not be afraid for the terror by night; nor for the arrow that flieth by day;

Nor for the pestilence that walketh in darkness; nor for the destruction that wasteth at noonday.

A thousand shall fall at thy side, and ten thousand at thy right hand; but it shall not come nigh thee.

Only with thine eyes shalt thou behold and see the reward of the wicked.

Because thou hast made the Lord, which is my refuge, even the most High, thy habitation;

There shall no evil befall thee, neither shall any plague come nigh thy dwelling.

For he shall give his angels charge over thee, to keep thee in all thy ways.

They shall bear thee up in their hands, lest thou dash thy foot against a stone.

Thou shalt tread upon the lion and adder: the young lion and the dragon shalt thou trample under feet.

Because he hath set his love upon me, therefore will I deliver him: I will set him on high, because he hath known my name.

He shall call upon me, and I will answer him: I will be with him in trouble; I will deliver him, and honour him.

With long life will I satisfy him, and shew him my salvation.

~ ~ ~ ~ ~ ~

JEREMIAH 29:11-14
King James Version

"For I know the thoughts that I think toward you," saith the LORD, "thoughts of peace, and not of evil, to give you an expected end.

Then shall ye call upon me, and ye shall go and pray unto me, and I will hearken unto you.

And ye shall seek me, and find me, ye shall search for me with all your heart.

And I will be found of you," saith the LORD...

DAUGHTERS

Daughters are sweet with lots of spice.
These are the words that make them nice.
They are lovable and enjoyable, too.
My heart was wooed when I met you.

You light up my world with sunshine and smiles.
You know how to turn my dials.
Daughters are beautiful, like daisies flying free.
God made her especially for me.

WRONG VIBES

When people feel rejected, it establishes a sense of humiliation, frustration, and aggravation. You never know whose life you may have affected
with your vulgar insults.

Your vibes need adjusting; see, you are not trusting yourself. You belittle others to make yourself feel as if you own the world. In all truth, your vibes
need to go through a washing cycle.

Who am I? It's not important.
I keep vibes even and smooth.
I don't have time for you to be rude.

Please change; it's wrong what you do.
So you don't feel the pain you put others through.
Your vibes are hurtful; they dig deep.
I've been watching you for the last few weeks.
What if the jokes or laughs were about you?
I feel you wouldn't know what to do.

Please change swiftly; give thoughts to one's feelings.
You can be a better person who can become appealing.

TRIPPIN

I took a trip to that windy city;
that mean Chi-Town gets very windy.
When that plane rolled on the ground,
those gusty winds just knocked me down.
I ran fast to catch my hat;
I didn't know it would get windy like that.
Big Shoulders twirl and smack your face.
The windy city is quite a place.

I met celebrities in my hotel;
The Ritz Carlton staff treated me well.
The food was terrific everywhere that I dined.
The waiters were all so very kind.
The traffic is heavy every day of the week.
It's always busy. I didn't get sleep.

The sun is beautiful and pleasant on the eyes.
Plenty of activities when I rise.
There are skyscrapers, architecture,
and museums to see.
Big Shoulders Town is the place to be.

JEWELS & RAGS

I wondered why you thought of me as jewels;
you misinterpreted me for rags. Hands down, everybody, no
applause. You are the owner of two faces; the one you wear to
impress the crowd;
you treat me fantastic.
The other is wicked and cold as a stone;
it's not official when we're alone.

Jewels & rags have no comparison.
One is genuine; the other is embarrassing.
Jewels are shimmers of one's personality.
Rags are bags of irrationality.

For example, your outbursts and attacks.
Your rags are so heavy they weigh down my back.
You lost your backbone not long after birth.
Your senseless and heartless time is not worth
the rags you gave me that I thought were jewels.
I never thought a person could be so cruel.

So, I go without taking anything from you.
Like the end of my story, we are through!

THE SHUFFLED CARDS

The Ace rules the deck. She must be a woman. She's confident, intelligent, and knows how to move throughout the rest of the deck to keep all others in line.

Next is the King; not many cards can take his place or beat him; he lays down the laws the rest of the deck follows. He is the lion in the jungle; he's usually the final card that makes the difference.

The Queen answers to no one. She is brilliant, inquisitive, and has powers beyond anyone's belief.

Jack is the son of the queen and king. It would be nothing but lethal to bother Jack in any way; in other words, it is better to be his friend, not his enemy.

Joker is the killer of the game; he is pretty dangerous. He has no sense of time, feelings, or concept of anyone's life. You see, the Joker runs as if he's the star on the track field.

Two through ten are the Gatekeepers—soldiers, all the other numbers. Nothing can pass these soldiers unless permitted by the Queen or King.

The system of the cards works because every card knows and respects its position.

PHOTOS ON THE WALL

The photos on the wall should be rearranged periodically.
Don't let them get too comfortable
in the same spot for twenty years.

The photos can hear the screams of their ancestors.
So, mix them up and place them on the wall in another room.
Sometimes, the pictures whisper out your secrets, although the image caught by the lenses is not the accurate picture that other photos see. These walls have held scholars, children to adulthood, me, you,
and many more before us.

Don't be afraid; the walls have also held some criminals' faces
that no longer belong in this society.
I did not say they couldn't be born again.
I'm just saying our walls have been more than busy holding all these pictures. The frames are the various stages that make the photos dance.
They stay at the border of the photograph.

Sometimes, the image looks like it's smiling at me,
so I smile back. I suspect that photos will have cameras to record the things people can't see or say in the future. This will help unsolved cases that go cold.

LOVE WARMTH SOUL

You spoke of a love that is present and past.
Our love came from tears and pain.
One for all because all for one.

In a flash of a moment, our love would not last.
I still love you despite the stain.
The memories and years were so much fun.

You were most bitter alone in a class.
I, too, will accept some of the blame.
One for all and all for one.

Cheese, wine, and enjoying the smooth sound of jazz.
Our love was sweet in the rain.
The memories and years were lots of fun.

I was your soldier but withered like grass.
I felt the hurt in my veins.
One for all and all for one.

Our love was different, like a fumeless gas.
It was forceful like the speed of a train.
The memories and years were definitely fun.
One for all because all for one.

STARRY NIGHT OVER THE RHÔNE

Let not your eyes blink with worry and heights.
Mysterious visions of this starry night.

Glimmers shape beauty near and far.
You can reach out and touch a star.

Explosions relieve colors from Van Gogh's name.
Starry Night Rhône makes handsome the frame.

Streaks of visions surround Mother Earth.
Starry Night Rhône contributes to birth.

The brightness, the essence, brings forth love.
Nights over Rhône is saluting Starry Night above.

LET THERE BE LIGHT

Let there be light because the dark there
scared a boy with his dog; they tremble with fear.
There are no batteries or flashlights near.
Their eyes are glowing and begin to tear.
There are strange sounds
from the whistling of thunder.
Will the storm cease? I certainly wonder.

Rain and hail hit the window's shutters.
A boy with his dog hides under the covers.
Bam! The door slams. Dad is home!
The boy and the dog are no longer alone.

The boy is happy. The dog grabs his bone.
Let there be light in this peaceful, sweet home.
Suddenly, the lights come back on.

HE ROSE AGAIN

They hung Him high as they pierced His soul
—no remorse for man.
The clouds turned cold in the sky
as they stabbed his feet and hands.
One drop of blood, minds grew weary;
they couldn't change what they'd done.
Somewhere in the Romans' jealously...
They've killed our Father's Son.

A mother helplessly cries out in pain
as her son's life leaves the earth.
All the believers show sorrow;
the Romans have no self-worth.

The Romans laugh as they sit on their horses
to tempt the Son of God.
When His head dropped, the Romans assumed
it was a final nod.

Suddenly, the rain, winds, and sky grew dark
while the storm blew out of control.
The Romans trembled at their actions.
My Father took control.

They were most frightened as they rode off;
they didn't look back again.
One of the Romans hollered,
"Was that the Son of Man?"

Three days later, in the cave,
the stone was rolled away.
The body of Christ has risen.
This is Resurrection Day!

YESTERYEARS

I am old but once was young.
Memories bring back so much fun.
I laugh, but then I cry;
some memories get trapped inside.
I will name these yesteryears:
a life that brings smiles and tears.

I struggle and hope to remember;
that part of my mind, I had to surrender.
It comes and goes whenever it likes;
it's sort of like an ongoing fight.
I have a daughter and also a son;
yesteryears are not over.

They've just begun.

SONNET: LOVE B

Is it not of me to be selfish?
Great love only works when you try.
You make excuses. You're helpless.
I spent many hours trying to get by.

Sunrises are beautiful, but not all alone.
You must be new to this; it's okay.
When it's dusk, the darkest hour, I roam.
Our friendship is too much work. I may not stay.

Butterflies communicate; their spots never change.
You are not in this alone.
You try, then you quit. This is strange.
We agreed to make a happy home.

Maybe we can scrap this; then try our love again.
Soul search our hearts; it lies deep within.

SONNET: BY MOUTH

When a woman of race makes a statement,
The world asks the question: "Why?"
Their boots are uncomfortable on this pavement.
The blisters on my feet make me cry.

Choirs sing chords while birds sing songs.
Hold your hand up if you've ever been wrong.
Twist of faith holds up my pen.
Hollering loud, "Do not sin!"

Reinstatement brings a cleansed new soul.
Live in this world that's careless and cold.
Women make statements as successful as men.
Walking proudly with high heels, hold up your chin.

They understood, and then worked it all out.
Please pass it on. It's by "word of mouth."

BLAZE CHAISE

Ghetto boys fly.
Point in the eye.
Look at the sky.
We real tough.
We get rough.
We talk stuff.
We sing praise.
We get raised.
We rephrase blasé.

THE TENANT

The woman upstairs is suspicious.
Visitors go up there but never come down.
Some may think I'm ridiculous.

She watches movies that are superstitious.
The visitors are too quiet; they don't make a sound.
The woman upstairs is suspicious.

The food she prepares smells delicious.
After eating, the guests are never around.
Some may think I'm ridiculous.

I know she cooks nutritious.
I pray the next guest does *not* back down.
The woman upstairs is suspicious.

The woman upstairs is vicious.
I wonder if her guest is from this town.
Some might say I'm ridiculous.

I hope she realizes I'm hip to this.
Guests go up and never come down.
The woman upstairs is vicious.
She's sneaky, plus suspicious.

STARSTRUCK

Wide hips with perfect lips.
Shoulders tall; waist is small.
Lashes are inviting. She's that exciting!
Confident and sure; she's far from bored.
You'll adore and want her more.

She's lovely and intriguing;
conversation she's receiving.
She is accepted by the majority.
What gives her this kind of authority?
Is it the hype, the people, and the fame?
It no longer excites her; it's all a shame.

She is starstruck, and can't love a soul.
Her attitude is awful; her heart is cold.
But unfortunately,
the world covers up the truth to be told.
They conceal the boundary
and then treat her like gold.

She's no fool.
She lives to survive people who know her claims.
She connives and deprives.
Most don't believe it
because she won't let you get close.
Her guard is up. She stands her post.

She is starstruck and couldn't care less if you agree. Starstruck is the title that sets her free.

FUNCTIONS

Dysfunctional, dismayed, thinking of the time when actuality
speaks the truth.
You don't like me, and I don't like you.
You can call me Black; however, if you say it, it lacks.
I can call myself White;
nevertheless, if *you* say it, it's not right.

Two different races in two unlike communities.
Some have none or more opportunities.
Gay and transgender people are a part of this.
It's none of your business what their sexual choice is.

Dysfunctional, dismayed, thinking of a time
when the reset button gets pushed now.
I wanted to push the button forty years ago.
Bragging on someone else's money won't buy you
that house you keep passing off the throughway.
Steve Harvey just bought Tyler Perry's castle.
Now, that is some accomplishment.
Congrats to you both.

To all the hip-shakers, the money-makers, and the
money-takers. I know they're in every race.
Not all people are bad, but they disgrace every race.
So how could you point your finger
and call *me* dysfunctional?

What gets me is that you are entirely comfortable.
Are there some Bill Cosbys who haven't gotten caught?
I mean, did Reynhard Sinaga use date-rape drugs
to assault men?
Why are drugs such as this even sold?
The pharmaceutical companies don't know;
they do what they're told.

Is this the truth or a bunch of vicious lies?
This misery goes past a needle in the eye.
Emmit Till's mother had a right to cry.
I'm exhausted from this because... All Lives Matter.
They were supposed to be climbing,
yet were falling down the ladder.

We have knees on necks, whips on trees,
the bodies being lynched.
God help us, please!

Things are messed up and out of control.
Did Jussie Smollett have whispers of lies that he told?
Should we believe him? The evidence shows the truth.
Why in the world would you do what you do?

Consequences are brutal.
They always come back.
They turn full circle and fall in your lap.

~ ~ ~ ~ ~ ~

GOD IS COMING BACK

God's re-collection of us is disappointing.
He gave us His Son; we ruined the anointing.
Brother against brother, a daughter against mother.
This foolishness wouldn't happen
if you genuinely loved her.

God is coming back; you better be ready!
God is coming back; you better tell your family.
With all power in His hands. God has a plan.
Are you ready, or is your head in the sand?

God is waiting to forgive your sin.
You need to trust Him so He can fulfill His plan.

THE SILENCE OF TIME

As time keeps ticking, she looks back many years at the world as compared to now. Her mind comes and goes now and then. She remembers her friends and refuses to believe they've gone on to a better place. Some people think she's old. She is brilliant in her secret little way. She peeks at her little watch every couple of seconds as if she were expecting company. With the mind of a scientist, you should never underestimate her.

A present comes in the mail for her; she opens it anxiously to find a large clock that ticks loudly. One thing she did not like was a watch or clock that she could hear. She loves to gaze at her watch, which does not make a sound—the silence of time.

By mistake only, she knocked the big clock onto the floor. When she picked it up, it was still working okay. However, she could no longer hear the ticking. As she looks at her clock, she jumps up quickly to put some breadcrumbs on the windowsill for the four birds that fly there every day. Be that as it may, she wondered if two of the birds were her two friends that passed away. She giggled and said, "No," because she did not believe in reincarnation.

Her head nods, and she jerks to find herself falling asleep. She wakes up and simultaneously rushes into the same routine she has followed for years.

FRIENDS SPEAK

Oprah Winfrey told Maya Angelou that these girls were wearing their pants too far off their hips. It seems that they can get more respect if they reveal less.

Maya Angelou states that the young men are also wearing "too low" pants. No respect for anyone.

Oprah says, "The world has changed drastically, Maya, I agree. People have become lovers of themselves. They don't fear God, and don't forget, prayer was removed from the schools."

"Oprah, that would explain all the threats, fights, and crimes. We will continue to pray about this subject."

"Well, Maya, some adults show irate behavior," says Oprah. "Could this be where our teenagers are learning it from?"

Maya says, "Your best friend, Gayle, couldn't have a better friend. You are a gift; you are God sent.

Oprah, I pray for this world and hope it gets better. You hear that gas is over seven dollars? Yes, the taxpayers and all of us who purchase gas are mixed up in a mess we didn't create!

I love you, Oprah. That's all I can say."

IT'S HER RIGHT

She has strolled through battlefields with souls that opposed her very presence. She beat down the hideous shadows. She once was afraid and felt she was fighting a losing battle. The nerve of her to want you to believe in her when she doesn't believe in herself.

She has no mirrors in her house because the reflection would wound her, depress her, and harass her. You said she sounded like she should be on medication. She never told you, but she has been taking twelve pills, three times a day, for the last three years. She will far exceed pain, stress, and worry. Marks peek through her make-up. Hair pieces and wigs covered her scalp, where hair once ran long down her back.

She tells me:

> "You are my friend, nevertheless; with all due respect, it is my right *not* to fight. I'm so tired of the radiation; it makes me so sick. I just never complained.
>
> Your fear will pass, and I will become a memory in your mind. The tough times will be fading soon. My destination still lives.
>
> You are my best friend; be that it may, it is still my right to give up this fight! One day, you will understand. However, it was always my right *not* to fight!"

IN DEATH'S DOORWAY

Have you ever met someone who told you they died and came back? Or they've seen a glimpse of heaven? If the answer is no, consider yourself meeting me.

My name is Cindy, nicknamed *Sparkle*. I just want to share a story with you. It is quite an experience; exposure to the other side. I woke up one day, realizing things didn't seem right. My surroundings were dissimilar, altered, and not the same. I didn't hear the birds singing.

My body was at peace; I felt light as a feather. My blood pressure did not bother me; I felt like I could fly—not on a plane. I was *not* dreaming, people. Things I despised, I suddenly liked. It didn't take forty-five minutes to do my hair; somebody had already done it. I was at perfect peace, although I could not recall where I was. I knew I wanted to remain here forever.

I understood that no harm could come to me here. I had no fear of anything. There were no regrets. I heard the most beautiful gospel singing that anyone could ever hear. The trees and grass here moved to the beat of the music, slow and smooth.

When I looked down, I witnessed clouds that were thick and bubbly—pure as the morning snow—but not cold. Thick golden streets, miles and miles away, I saw angels everywhere. They were pleasant, enjoyable, and welcoming. There were no old family members or friends reminding me of what I couldn't do. I didn't remember my past, and this place was amusing. I felt so good about myself there. I loved everyone, and I could feel their love back.

I know we've all heard the saying, "I must have died and gone to heaven." Well, somehow, my body was in between a debate. I was in that part of my life where a decision had to be made. Somehow, I could feel everyone's heart; it was warm, peace was at hand, and life was grand. The hell I left couldn't pull me back with twenty bulldozers! In death's doorway, I had to choose. That's how things are.

When I stood at the door, I could feel my soul dropping down fast before hitting bottom; I was swept off my feet by perhaps an angel. Scenes of my life flashed before me in five-year segments:

At five, I saw myself meeting my father at the naval base; he was coming home from the Navy. I had on my pretty pink dress.

Next, I was ten. I got chased home from school by bullies. I was so afraid of them.

Then, I was fifteen years old and walking to school. The old lady in front of me dropped a fifty-dollar bill. I picked it up and made plans to spend it for myself. At this part of my life, I was shown that this was the woman's last bit of money for her medicine, cat food, and groceries. I felt terrible at that moment. I had made the wrong decision.

In death's doorway, I walked through!
I can't tell you any more from this point.

Until your day comes to walk through the door...
if you get the opportunity to walk through.

DAY AT THE LIBRARY

I don't want to live in this world another day!

My computer is on the bum again, so I am going to the library. *"EEK!"* I forgot my flash drive.

It seems as if I'm going to have a bad day. I scan the room suspiciously; as a matter of fact, it's hot, crowded, and noisy. *What is it, Children's Day or something?* I thought to myself. *Where are the children's parents?* Then, *Bam!* "There goes a small bookshelf with books and flyers falling everywhere. The bookshelf almost fell on one of the children in a matter of seconds.

The librarian zooms over to ensure none of the boys are hurt; she escorts the three boys back to their seats. She examined the room; her expression said, *where are the children's parents?* At the desk across from me, I keep hearing this knocking sound. *Is this happening?* This man is knocking on the table abruptly and making sucking sounds with his mouth as if trying to make a rap song. *Hello, Sir, this is a library.* I did not say that out loud; however, I sure wanted to.

Who bought their kids here to chase each other all over the place? I'm looking behind the counter where three people are working! No one is saying anything. I believe they are afraid to say something to the parents, who, by the way, are nowhere to be found. Oh, no, there is one seat left, and it looks like the loud lady is coming right toward me to sit down. *Did I mention she is on her phone arguing with someone?* Sounds like her boyfriend. This lady has used every unpleasant word in the book.

I finally screamed out loud, "This is a library, not a place to be rude!" No one is respecting anyone here! (Lady on the phone says, "You better not hang up on me. Hello, hello, are you there?" The lady hollers out, "He hung up on me!" Finally, a worker asked the lady to silence her cell phone. The lady's shoulders rose, the head went back slightly to the side, eyes looking over her glasses. Mouth poked out. She looked at the librarian, and I thought she would hit her.

The weaselly man working behind the counter did not come over to say anything! The lady hollered at the librarian with the loudest words ever! "He's lucky my phone is dead! I'm going to kick his..." Well, you know the rest.

The two little kids are chasing each other in the library (sister and brother). Their mother just bought them each a Happy Meal; this made them a little quieter while the huge sign on the wall clearly states, "No Eating in the Library." *That's it, Lady!* I had to go to the counter to say something. I tell the guard I can't concentrate because there is too much noise in this library.

"Do you see the kids who were chasing each other? Now they're eating their McDonald's. The sign states no eating in here. Why won't you say anything to their parents?"

The guard replies, "They don't listen to us; they want to argue."

I asked, why don't you call the police to assist you?"

The guard explains, "The last time I called the police, my car ended up with pink and purple paint all over it."

"You're kidding," I said.

"I'm not, and I could not press charges because the camera did not pick up who did it.

You know, I've seen better days than this. No one, including the children, is following the library's rules. This opens the door for disrespect to each other. This world we live in isn't perfect. However, what kind of world would this be if we did not have rules? We would be living in the wild, wild, west. I have been in the library for less than forty-five minutes, and at least seven major written rules seem to be invisible. Librarians are afraid to do their jobs because of retaliation. The children are too young to understand that you don't run and chase each other in the library.

The parents left their children to go purchase their Happy Meal. The lady is arguing with her boyfriend. *Come on, she knows better!* I can honestly speak for myself and a few others in the library. We do not care to hear your conversation with your boyfriend. You are rude to speak it out loud and not be courteous to others.

The man is hitting on the table, making strange loud sounds from his mouth. There are no books in front of him or paperwork. *Why is he even here?* This is not an audition for a contest; take that somewhere else. I gave him the worst look, and it did not even seem to bother him.

I don't want to live in this world another day without making a difference. I'm not going to complain anymore to the staff here. I'm simply going to go to a different library. My plan to make this problem better is to write the state governor and explain why all libraries should have trained security guards. But before I write the governor, I would like to do a little experiment. This will include me going to at least four other libraries and taking notes on the behavior of the other staff and people in the library. Hopefully, this will stop disrespectful people from coming into the library, treating it as a social club or daycare center.

The behaviors go on for an hour, and the children's parents... *wait, guess who just arrived here?* A parent. I don't know; I must wear my feelings on my face because here comes their mother right toward me.

"I know I'm a stranger to you," she says. "I need to ask you a huge favor."

I point to myself and give her a questioning look.

"Yes, you. Can you please give me a ride? I have a job interview in thirty minutes. My boyfriend won't take me, and I need this job."

I asked her, "Where will your children go while you're interviewing?

"Oh, that's the second part of the favor I wanted to ask you," she says. "Can they sit in the car with you for a few minutes?"

"I don't know," I say. "We don't know each other."

"Hello, my name is Tabatha. I have four sons I'm trying to feed. What is your name?"

"I'm Sallyanne."

"Pleased to meet you, Sallyanne. Can you please do me this favor?"

"There's no one else you can ask?"

"No."

"Okay, I'll do it. Hopefully, the children are tired from all that running they did when you were gone," I say.

Tabatha says, "Yes, the children will most likely go to sleep. Thank you so much."

I'll say it here for the last time: "I don't want to live in this world another day and not make a difference."

~ ~ ~ ~ ~ ~

THE EXPERIMENT

I dressed very poorly and went into a restaurant in Amherst; I will not mention the name.

I went over to the counter so I could be seated, and a group of people dashed in front of me. The hostess ushered them to their table, skipping me. I sighed while making a few noises to let them know that this was unacceptable.

I had on cut-off pants, a torn, raggedy shirt, and mismatched socks (one purple and one orange). My hair looked terrible; my coat was grimy and too small. I could tell that no one wanted to seat me or talk to me because they probably thought I was a bum.

Finally, I asked, "Can I be seated, please?"

The hostess stated, "We'll be right with you."

After watching several other people being seated instead of me, I eased out the door.

After going home for a few hours, I returned to the restaurant. I looked fantastic—from head to toe—and intended to make a statement. I wore all name-brand clothing and an expensive Chanel handbag on my arm. None of the servers had a clue that I was that *bum* who had left a few hours ago. This time, the service was out of sight! Not surprisingly, I was seated immediately. I even skipped three people who were already waiting. The gestures and expressions of the people waiting did not surprise me; they were not happy and felt this was unfair.

The waitress, according to her name tag, was Shavonn. She poured me a *sample* of cabernet, filling half the glass. From a table across from me, I heard a woman whisper, "You didn't pour *me* that much for *my* sample."

Shavonn ignored her. She went to the back, where the food was being prepared. I watched as a few employees gathered, looking my way.

One young lady approached and asked, "Is that a real Chanel bag?"

I spoke as if I was not from this part of the world. With a British accent, I said, "Why sure, it's natural. I wouldn't get caught alive with a fake handbag."

A few moments later, I heard a different employee say, "You shouldn't have asked her that!"

After finishing my meal, I left my waitress an eight-dollar tip. From the look on her face, she expected more.

The moral of this story is to treat everyone the same.

~ ~ ~ ~ ~ ~

BURNING SECRET

Your secret you told me—it burns in my chest.
I weep, and I cry and never get rest.
I toss and turn and then think of you.
I know you did it; just wish it weren't true.

Years have passed, and it haunts me the same.
You live life normally while others take blame.
Your secret burns and brings me to stress.
I hate that you involved me in this mess.

How can I fix the damage? It is deep.
I yearn to get just one good night's sleep.
I don't understand how this can be;
You do dirt, and it falls on me.

I rot in here while you see the sun.
I feel like running to tell everyone.
This secret that burns... it hurts my head.
I hate to say it, but I wish I were dead.

I never thought I'd be in this place.
A beautiful life. What a waste!
Look at you, just grinning with glee.
I'd like to trade places... to again be free.

You trapped me with promises and lies untrue.
The people who love you—if they only knew.
You can go to mass and hail Mary all night;
 your secret will one day come to light.

Everyone will see that you're not real.
Then you'll know just how I feel.
I hope you sleep really well at night.
I know your dreams are a pitiful sight.

You're fake, and phony, and very untrue.
I *still* ask God to please forgive you.

~ ~ ~ ~ ~ ~

BURNING SECRET
Reflections

1. What do you suppose the secret is in this poem?

2. Do you think it is a woman talking to a man or a man talking to a woman?

3. Do you think the wrong person has been incarcerated?

4. Do you think the two characters in this poem were once involved?

A FATHER'S BETRAYAL

The "rage-full" nights, the hollering fights!
No good stories about my "Dad."
Mama prayed, but then she stayed.
No good stories. Yes, this is sad.
Many times, I prayed to God
to take us out of this situation,
but I felt He didn't listen,
and it made me more frustrated!

The "glareless" stare to a place unknown
is where you'd often find me.
It had become my comfort zone,
a getaway to help unwind me.
Love and peace she never felt;
instead, it was anger and rage.
I played the part like it never happened,
like I was an actor on a stage.

I "saw" the love in his eyes;
he showed my sister and brother;
However, when you got down to it,
he hated me and my mother.
As the years went on, the abuse continued
—physical, verbal, and mental.
Finally, I asked a question of the sky,
"How could he be so sinful?"

My poor mother, for forty years,
waiting to be his bride.
All those years of lust and lies;
even so, he had something to hide.
Another son! From a different mother,
Guess that makes him my brother.
I looked to the sky and asked,
"Did this man ever love my mother?"

Now I have a brother I have never met,
and this is not his or my fault.
How can my father ever teach
when he can never be taught?
Twenty years of his drinking and weed
and company staying late at night.
Most decisions that he made
were very seldom right.

I could go on telling the story;
as a result, it makes me tearful.
I choose to walk away, right now today,
to keep my spirit cheerful.

~ ~ ~ ~ ~ ~

A FATHER'S BETRAYAL
Reflections

1. Do you think it is obvious this character did not care for their father?

2. At what point did the character explain why they did not value their father?

3. Did you feel the character speaking is the only one the father treats unfairly?

4. Did the main character solve their problem or come to a conclusion?

~ ~ ~ ~ ~ ~

RESTAURANT ZERO

"Would you eat your dinner with rats?"

I spotted rat droppings on the floor near the kitchen; nevertheless, I know the difference between rat turds and peppercorns! I'm finishing up the last of my dinner. I walked over to the kitchen to advise the waiter that she had forgotten my water. I see a slinky older man with three freckles on each cheek. His pants are saggy; his shirt is dingy white; he has enormous black shoes; the older man strolls; I can see he's tired with little energy. The older man's name tag reads Harvey Kinkel.

My server is Harriet. Her eyes meet mine as she massages and rubs her feet. Harriet quickly jumps to her feet and makes her way to the sink. Harriet takes her bare hands and fills six glasses with ice. I'm in disbelief that Harriet did not wash her hands since she needed to touch the ice to serve it. I believe Mr. Harvey is making her nervous; in addition, Harriet is all over the place. My eyes do a quick scan of the kitchen. The back door was open for air, although it was about 95 degrees. The screen has a huge hole that allows flies and insects to fly in, and the dishwasher has a sign that emphasizes it's broken.

Dishes are piled a mile high in some dirty dishwater; the wall is greasy and dull, and needless to say, no one washes it! Mr. Harvey comes into the kitchen from outside with a kangaroo on a leash. He rushes to tie the leash on a nail sticking out of the wall. Next, he came over to the door and advised me that I could not be near the kitchen! Mr. Harvey gives me a little shove back toward the dining area. I yell, "Hey, you can't have an animal in the kitchen! I saw the rat turds too!"

Harriet rushes past me so fast that she drops a hot pepper out of a bowl of salad; she picks it up with her bare hands and throws it back in the salad. Harriet is the only one working fifteen tables. I can't let her serve that salad or six glasses of water to customers. I know it's a rough night for Mr. Harvey and Harriet; nevertheless, people deserve dignity. I purposely bump into Harriet, causing her to drop everything. I explain to Harriet, and I am so sorry. Harriet's hands go up in the air with ice water, and salads are everywhere.

All of this is making me sick to my stomach. I rush off to the men's room. I hear a customer in the bathroom on the phone saying, "The food here is excellent. I will bring you next week." To think, I couldn't wait to eat here for the first time. I give this restaurant a big fat zero!

There is a loud commotion outside of the restroom. Several Department of Health officers abruptly rushed into the restaurant to advise all employees that the restaurant would be closed down. I'm not surprised; this restaurant failed so many regulations. Although several letters, in fact, all, were ignored by Mr. Kinkle. One of the Department's head workers seems intrigued, taping signs on the restaurant's glass closed until further notice.

Mr. Harvey is so sad. I hate seeing him this way. He pointed to me and asked that I call his employees in the blue book on the kitchen shelf and advise them that the restaurant is being closed down. Next, Mr. Harvey asked that I take the kangaroo. I point out that I have no room for an animal of his size, plus I can't take care of him. Finally, Mr. Harvey asked me to take him to the city zoo.

"I will miss him," Mr. Harvey stated with tearful eyes.

I went into the kitchen and sat at a broken-down old desk to call Mr. Harvey's employees. There must be twenty-five employees in this phone book; why are only two people working tonight? I can clearly say that Mr. Harvey let his employees get away with excuses.

First call:

"Hello, can I speak to Mr. Verrado?"

"This is he."

"Mr. Verrado, this is Restaurant Zero calling to advise you that the restaurant is being shut down.

"What? Why? Where is Mr. Harvey?"

"He's talking to authorities."

"I will come in tomorrow, I promise."

"Don't bother."

"Where is the kangaroo?" asked Mr. Verrado.

"I will take him to the city zoo. I'm sorry, Mr. Verrado, I have several other employees to call. It all comes down to this: You have to take your next job seriously."

~ ~ ~ ~ ~ ~

RESTAURANT ZERO
Reflections

1. Why do you suppose the first sentence in this story was in bold?

2. Do you feel it was fair that Mr. Harvey and Harriet were working alone?

3. Would you agree that Mr. Harvey let his employees take advantage of him?

4. Did you think that you would have taken in a kangaroo?

HOPE

H is for *help*.
We're asking God to take us out of this hell.

O is for *overall*.
We're all suffering in some form.
Some people in silence?
The beginning of self-destruction looks like this.

P is for *pain*,
which switched places with progress.
Now we're right back to hurt—
sharp, aching, throbbing, senseless deaths.

E is for *effective* change.
This must happen before it's too late.

H is for *hollering*.
As loud as I can. Do you hear me?

O is for *overwhelmed*.
We're all feeling overload right about now.

P is for *patience*.
We will pray and wait, then pray and wait some more. Most of us know whose we are.

E is for *effort*.
To come to an understanding that shall help us all.

Or will it be *egotistic* brainstorming that has destroyed and drained life?

Boastful, opinionated, selfish verses. We have faith.

THE MARQUIS WHO'S WHO PUBLICATIONS BOARD

is pleased to recognize

SONYA DANIELS-HINES

as a recipient of the

Albert Nelson Marquis Lifetime Achievement Award

an honor reserved for Marquis Biographees who have achieved career longevity and demonstrated unwavering excellence in their chosen fields.

Erica Lee
President

2021